Santa
from
Cincinnati

Peter & Barbara Claus

proudly announce

the arrival of their son,

born December 25,

weighing 7 lbs., 2 oz.

Dedicated to Elf C
—J. B.

To Kim, Chad, Brad, and Kelli.
And many thanks to Dvorah Governale
for her expert research and professional costume design.
—K. H.

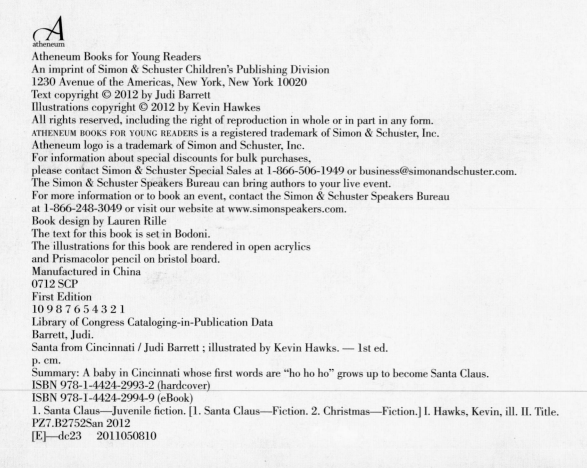
Atheneum Books for Young Readers
An imprint of Simon & Schuster Children's Publishing Division
1230 Avenue of the Americas, New York, New York 10020
Text copyright © 2012 by Judi Barrett
Illustrations copyright © 2012 by Kevin Hawkes
All rights reserved, including the right of reproduction in whole or in part in any form.
ATHENEUM BOOKS FOR YOUNG READERS is a registered trademark of Simon & Schuster, Inc.
Atheneum logo is a trademark of Simon and Schuster, Inc.
For information about special discounts for bulk purchases,
please contact Simon & Schuster Special Sales at 1-866-506-1949 or business@simonandschuster.com.
The Simon & Schuster Speakers Bureau can bring authors to your live event.
For more information or to book an event, contact the Simon & Schuster Speakers Bureau
at 1-866-248-3049 or visit our website at www.simonspeakers.com.
Book design by Lauren Rille
The text for this book is set in Bodoni.
The illustrations for this book are rendered in open acrylics
and Prismacolor pencil on bristol board.
Manufactured in China
0712 SCP
First Edition
10 9 8 7 6 5 4 3 2 1
Library of Congress Cataloging-in-Publication Data
Barrett, Judi.
Santa from Cincinnati / Judi Barrett ; illustrated by Kevin Hawks. — 1st ed.
p. cm.
Summary: A baby in Cincinnati whose first words are "ho ho ho" grows up to become Santa Claus.
ISBN 978-1-4424-2993-2 (hardcover)
ISBN 978-1-4424-2994-9 (eBook)
1. Santa Claus—Juvenile fiction. [1. Santa Claus—Fiction. 2. Christmas—Fiction.] I. Hawks, Kevin, ill. II. Title.
PZ7.B2752San 2012
[E]—dc23   2011050810

Judi Barrett

Santa
from
Cincinnati

illustrated by
Kevin Hawkes

ATHENEUM BOOKS FOR YOUNG READERS ✦ New York Toronto London Sydney New Delhi

NAME: *Perkes*

NAME: *López*

NAME: *Gong*

$\mathbb{I}$ was born Baby Boy Claus at 12:02 AM at the Cincinnati General Hospital on December 25, many, many, many years ago.

My parents had trouble deciding on
the perfect name for me, but finally
found just the right one . . .
in their soup.

First teeth

First words: "ho, ho, ho"

First steps

I was their first and their only child. So they took a lot of pictures of me.

I was a pretty good baby. Didn't cry too much. Ate. Pooped. Peed. Slept . . . sometimes.

I was jolly and roly-poly and had rosy cheeks from day one. The doctor diagnosed me with "a jovial disposition."

I went through milestones just like most other babies. But mine were a little different.

My obsession with toys started early. I played
with them for hours. My favorite one was
a stuffed reindeer. In fact, since I liked it so much,
my mother got me several more.

I took them everywhere.
She gave me a pillowcase
to carry them around in.

Around age five, I started wearing
a fake beard and mustache, so I could look
just like my dad. My teacher didn't know
quite what to make of it, but my classmates
were amused.

I had the most clever dad. He made all my toys in his basement workshop. They were the best toys in all of Cincinnati. I couldn't wait till I was old enough to help.

When I was ten, my dad gave me my first set of professional tools.

I made an amazingly elaborate toy
that impressed him so much, he decided
to give me the keys to the workshop . . .
with one rule: I had to do my homework first!

The neighborhood kids liked to watch us
through the window and asked if we could
make some toys for them.

So we did . . . for their birthdays, special occasions, and holidays. We got so many requests that we started keeping lists. They grew longer and longer every day.

playing guitar in a rock band

SANTA AND HIS REINDEER

My mom felt it was important
that I had other interests as well,
so she kept me pretty busy.

I also tried my hand at various
part-time jobs to earn some money.

playing third base

My first tip! 25¢!

My first broken plate! 25¢!! :(

Babysitting

Waiting tables at the local luncheonette

I invented a cannon-type of toy that shot newspapers right smack onto people's doorsteps. It worked like a dream, and I was very proud of it!

Report Ca

French   A
German   A
Spanish   A
Italian   A
Latin   A
English   B

Delivering newspapers

Then one day, right before my birthday, I realized I had too many toys—thousands too many—and I didn't have room for one more.

So, I came up with a clever plan.
I would deliver one of my toys to every
child in Cincinnati on Christmas Eve.

My mom and dad helped me load them onto some sleds I'd tied together. Just as I was about to leave, I found more toys under my bed. So I stuffed those into my pillowcase, flung it over my shoulder, and I was off!

The night was a huge success. The children were so happy with their toys that I decided to make it an annual event (though I needed to find a more efficient way to get around).

Soon children from all over Ohio were sending me lists of toys they wanted for Christmas.

However, I still managed to:

get my homework done,

get my driver's license,

fill out college applications,

go to the senior prom,

and think about what I wanted to be when I grew up.

DANCE CARD

STUDENT: SANTA CLAUS

ART   A+

SCIENCE   A+

READING   A+

GEOGRAPHY A+++

ENGLISH   A+

SOCIAL
STUDIES   A+

MATH   C

I got accepted to a very unusual college where they let me major in toys and minor in business. It was far, far away from Cincinnati, but I've always liked cold weather.

It was the perfect place for me. I made loads of amazing toys and lots of amazing friends, including the future Mrs. Claus.

Word spread and children all around the world started hearing about my once-a-year toy deliveries. I started getting mail from, well, everywhere! This kept me busier than ever.

When my mom and dad came to visit, they were very proud of me, but slightly horrified. I clearly needed a better system.

I was able to shorten my list of toy recipients by finding out who was naughty and who was nice and making two separate lists. That cut down a bit on the number of toys I needed.

My new friends volunteered to help, but still, it turned out to be the biggest Christmas Eve delivery I'd ever done!

The elves were no match for a full sled,
so I enlisted the help of some local reindeer.
They, along with more than a little Christmas
magic, got things moving.

It was yet another successful
Christmas Eve.

Just as successful were my final months at college. By the time I got my diploma, there were so many toys that there wasn't enough room for them anywhere.

For a wedding present, the future Mrs. Claus started looking for a place with more space where we could settle down.

We consulted a real-estate agent. He showed us various possibilites . . .

Raccoon in residence!

Hats off to Graduation Day

Who caught the mistletoe?

. . . and finally found the perfect one
for us. It had lots and lots of rooms
and best of all, central heating.

After we moved in and fixed up the place,
I made a big sign to put above the front door.
And I put a different one in a window.
I had a huge response and was able to
give jobs to lots of people.

And you know the rest of the story. . . .

Today my workshop is thriving. We have
to make toys almost every day
of the year in order to keep
up with demands.

I'm jollier, my cheeks have gotten rosier, and my
belly has grown a bit more rotund with each year.

Mrs. Claus helps out in many ways, and she
even perfected my special Santa suit.

And best of all, I now have a large, jet-propelled sleigh that gets me around the world in a jiffy and makes it less tiring for the reindeer. And thanks to my GPS, we never ever get lost.

Life just couldn't be merrier!

xoxo,
Claus & Co.